For Paloma —
I will love you forever. —
G.G.J.

P9-DMU-780

# Forever

Emma Dodd

templar books

an imprint of Candlewick Press

When you're happy, having fun,
I feel happy, too.

When you giggle, play, and run,
I laugh along with you.

. I do my best to cheer you up
when you are feeling down . . .

to see if I can make you smile
and smooth away your frown.

If you're ever feeling scared,
I'll be right beside you.

If you're ever feeling lost,
know that I will find you.

When you share your
hopes and wishes,
I'll keep them safe for you . . .

and promise to do all I can
to make those dreams come true.

And no matter what may come as
we journey on together . . .

know that
deep within my heart,
I will love you . . .

forever.

Copyright © 2013 by Emma Dodd

All rights reserved. No part of this book may be reproduced,
transmitted, or stored in an information retrieval system
in any form or by any means, graphic, electronic,
or mechanical, including photocopying, taping, and recording,
without prior written permission from the publisher.

First U.S. edition 2013

Library of Congress Catalog Card Number 2013943157
ISBN 978-0-7636-7132-7

17 18 LEO 10 9 8 7

Printed in Heshan, Guangdong, China

This book was typeset in Eureka Sans.
The illustrations were created digitally.

TEMPLAR BOOKS

an imprint of
Candlewick Press
99 Dover Street
Somerville, Massachusetts 02144
www.candlewick.com